To every child who sees the world
a little differently
— A.S.

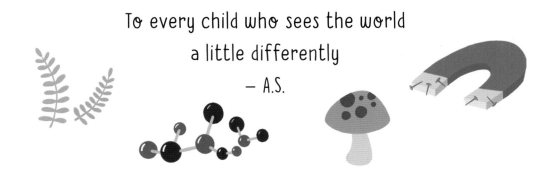

Tundra Books, an imprint of Penguin Random House Canada Young Readers,
a division of Penguin Random House of Canada Limited

Library and Archives Canada Cataloguing in Publication

Title: Solid, liquid, gassy : a fairy science story / Ashley Spires.
Names: Spires, Ashley, 1978– author.
Description: Series statement: Fairy science
Identifiers: Canadiana (print) 20190236485 | Canadiana (ebook) 20190236493
ISBN 9780735264274 (hardcover) | ISBN 9780735264281 (EPUB)
Classification: LCC PS8637.P57 S65 2020 | DDC jC813/.6—dc23

Published simultaneously in the United States of America by Crown Books for Young Readers,
an imprint of Penguin Random House LLC, New York

Edited by Phoebe Yeh and Tara Walker
The artwork in this book was rendered digitally, sprinkled with sparkles, and frozen solid.

Printed and bound in China

www.penguinrandomhouse.ca

1   2   3   4   5   24   23   22   21   20

tundra | Penguin
Random House
TUNDRA BOOKS

FAIRY SCIENCE
SOLID, LIQUID, GASSY

Ashley Spires

tundra

Esther does not believe in magic.
Which is kind of a big deal when you are a fairy.

How does Jack Frost make snow?

Magic!

While the other fairies wish on stars, Esther conducts experiments.

While they learn spells, she studies the law of density.

She's a fairy who prefers a microscope to a wand.

Esther is dedicated to science.
She and her friends use the scientific
method to explore the world around them.

First they ask a question.

What happens to ice when it warms up?

Then they do some research.

DON'T LICK IT!

They each make a hypothesis.

The ice will change color!

It will turn into liquid!

It will become a raspberry!

They do experiments, and they examine their results.

Finally they draw their conclusions.

Esther and her friends try to share their discovery at school, but none of their fairymates are interested.

So, as you can clearly see, the rising temperature causes the water to change from solid to liquid, which is the real reason the ice melts!

JOIN THE PIXIEVILLE SPRING MAGIC FAIR!

ICE + HEAT = MELT!

They are too busy planning for the Magic Fair to listen to her silly logical theories.

Now, Esther, we all know that moon sneezes are what make the ice disappear each spring.

Last year's fair didn't go well for Esther. It turns out magic enthusiasts are surprisingly clueless.

While her fairymates work on their magic projects,
Esther focuses on solving scientific problems.

How does the compass needle always point north?

Last one in the pond is a rotten toadstool!

And there is no bigger problem . . .

SPLOOOT!

. . . than a missing pond!

There are lots of ideas about what happened to the pond.

But only Esther and her science pals observe the facts.

Fig asks a question.

Where did the pond go?

Clover does some research.

This has been the hottest spring in years!

Esther forms a hypothesis.

We know water is a solid when it's very cold, and it turns to a liquid when it warms up. . . .

Together, they conduct experiments and examine the results.

At last, they draw their conclusion.

Since there is no scientific way to force it to rain, Esther and her friends just have to wait to see if her theory is correct.

I've noticed that science seems to involve a lot of waiting.

Come here, pondy pond!

They wait and wait and wait a little longer, until finally it starts to pour.

Eureka! They were right!
After a few days of steady rain,
the pond is restored.

My potion worked!

It's amazing that water
can change states like that.
No wonder some fairies
think it's magic.

Hmm . . .

The water cycle is
almost magical.

And that gives Esther the perfect way to bring science to the Magic Fair!

MAGIC FAIR TODAY!

COLORS AND THEIR MEANINGS

WHAT YOUR AURA SAYS ABOUT YOU!

PIXIE DUST: What Can't It Do?

HOW FATE WORKS: Why I Was MEANT to Write This Report

My Aunt TOOTH FAIRY: The Story of a Molar Hoarder

Has Esther finally made everyone excited about science?

The winner of this year's Magic Fair is . . .

Apparently, the Magic Fair isn't ready for science.
But the judges appreciate a good costume.

Esther, Clover, and Fig
get first place for
Best Magic Fair Costume Design!

BEST COSTUME

BEST COSTUME

BEST COSTUME

Esther may not have won any trophies, but like all good scientists,
she knows that discovery is the best reward.

And there is *always* something new to discover.

ESTHER'S RAINY-DAY EXPERIMENT

You don't have to be a fairy to do a science experiment! Why not make it rain indoors? You'll need these things:

Experiment Checklist

Hot Water
One Large Glass Bowl
Food Coloring
Salt
One Small Glass Cup
Plastic Wrap
Ice Cubes
Spoon

First, pour the hot water into the bowl so it is about a quarter full. Ask an adult for help.

Next, add food coloring and a pinch of salt to the water and give it a stir.

Place the small cup into the bowl. Be careful to keep the cup dry inside.

Quickly cover the bowl with plastic wrap and place a few ice cubes on top.